"Just one more question," said the policeman. SpongeBob stood there shaking, biting his nails, sure that the policeman was about to ask him if he'd thrown the peanut at Clamu. What would the punishment be for such a terrible crime?

"Is it true that you were at the oyster's lair with a Mr. Patrick Star?" asked the policeman.

"Yes!" wailed SpongeBob. "Yes! It's all true! The merriment! The peanut! The Patrick!" He fell to his knees, crying.

"That's all we need to know, son," said the policeman, satisfied. He turned to his partner. "Let's book him!"

Zoo Day DISASTER

by **David Lewman**

based on an original teleplay by

Paul Tibbitt, Walt Dohrn, and Mr. Lawrence

illustrated by **Robert Dress**

SCHOLASTIC INC.

New York Toronto London Auckland Sydney
Mexico City New Delhi Hong Kong Buenos Aires

Stephen Hillenburg (signature)

Based on the TV series *SpongeBob SquarePants*®
created by Stephen Hillenburg as seen on Nickelodeon®

ISBN 0-439-76097-6

12 11 10 9 8 7 6 5 4 3 2 1   5 6 7 8 9 10/0

Printed in the U.S.A.   08

First Scholastic printing, September 2005

Look for these other
SpongeBob SquarePants
chapter books!

chapter one

It was Annual Free Day at the Bikini Bottom Zoo. Just about everyone in town was at the zoo having fun—including SpongeBob's greedy boss, Mr. Krabs.

Mr. Krabs loved Free Day. On Free Day he could get all kinds of things without spending any of his beloved money.

Wearing a fake black mustache as a disguise, Mr. Krabs grabbed everything he could.

When a zoo employee handed out free balloons, Mr. Krabs took the whole bunch. At the free drink stand, he filled an entire barrel with soda. He even took lightbulbs right out of the zoo's sidewalk lamps!

"Top o' the mornin', boys!" said Mr. Krabs a little nervously when two Bikini Bottom policemen approached him. He was afraid they might recognize him as the guy who took advantage of Free Day every year.

"Whew!" he sighed as they walked on by without saying anything. My disguise must have fooled them, he thought.

"Next stop, gift shop!" he said. With his pockets full of hot dogs and lollipops, Mr. Krabs ran eagerly into the gift shop for more goodies.

SpongeBob didn't notice his Krusty Krab boss as he and his best friend, Patrick, headed for the zoo's magnificent Oyster Stadium. He was too excited about seeing Clamu, the giant oyster.

"Not only is he the largest oyster held in captivity," he explained to Patrick, "he also does tricks!"

SpongeBob took off his Free Day propeller beanie and spoke in a loud announcer's voice. "HE SPITS A GIANT PEARL ONE HUNDRED FEET IN THE AIR . . . LIKE A CANNONBALL!"

Now SpongeBob pretended to be the giant oyster. He wadded up his hat, stuffed it in his mouth, chewed a little, and spat the beanie high into the air. It landed with a *PLOP* right on

a little kid's ice-cream cone.

"Why are we hanging around watching a cheap imitation?" yelled Patrick, excitedly hopping from foot to foot. "Let's get over there!"

Panting, he and SpongeBob sprinted into Oyster Stadium shouting, "This is the greatest day of our lives!"

But when they reached the inside of the stadium and peered down into Clamu's arena, the giant oyster was sleeping soundly. He snored, opening his huge mouth and curling his shiny pink tongue. He sure wasn't doing any tricks.

"This is the greatest day of our lives?" asked Patrick, leaning on the red rope that kept visitors from falling into Clamu's pit. "Bo-ring!"

Clamu just kept snoring. Bubbles rose from his shell with every low, rumbling snore.

SpongeBob was disappointed, too. He'd told Patrick the giant oyster would be a sight to behold, and now it was just lying there, sleeping. "You're right, Patrick," he said. "We came to see"—SpongeBob switched back to his announcer's voice—"PEARLS ONE HUNDRED FEET IN THE AIR!" He pointed one yellow finger straight up toward the top of the stadium. Patrick smiled, agreeing with his friend.

"I'll try my oyster call," said SpongeBob. He raised his hands to his mouth and opened wide. "OOO-WAAA-LOO-LOO-LOO-LAA-WAA-LOO-WAAAAAA!" he cried, ending with a pathetic squeak.

Clamu just kept on snoring.

SpongeBob turned to Patrick helplessly. He'd given it his best shot, but his oyster call hadn't worked at all.

Patrick looked bored. "Well, I'm outta here," he said. "Thanks for nothing, SpongeBob."

As Patrick walked out of the stadium SpongeBob sadly watched his friend go. This day wasn't turning out the way he'd planned at all.

Free Day at the zoo was supposed to be fun, not boring. In fact, it was supposed to be the greatest day of their lives!

He knew he had to do *something* to save the day.

chapter two

SpongeBob stared down miserably at the giant oyster. "Come on, come on," he said. "Wake up, already." But Clamu kept snoring.

Then SpongeBob got an idea. He pulled a bag of sea peanuts out of his pocket. Then he picked out one small peanut, and looked around to see if anyone was watching. The coast was clear. He held the peanut high over his head, then whipped it at the giant oyster with a grunt.

It bounced harmlessly off the tough purple shell. Clamu stirred, then opened his mouth and made a puzzled sound.

SpongeBob was thrilled. "I think it's working!" he said, grinning. Clamu shifted around, first facing in one direction, then the other, then back to his original position.

"Hey, Patrick!" SpongeBob called. "Clamu is waking up!" Patrick ran back into the arena.

"Oh, boy!" he shouted. "Did I miss it?"

SpongeBob smiled. "No, the show's about to begin!" he said confidently.

SpongeBob was right about that. But the show wasn't exactly what he had in mind. Instead of performing dazzling tricks, Clamu threw open his gigantic mouth and let out the loudest sob anyone had ever heard!

"WAHHHHHH!" he cried.

Clamu's cry was so loud, it blew SpongeBob and Patrick off their feet. They had to cling

tightly to the red safety rope or they would have been blown right out of the arena.

As Clamu cried and leaped around his pit two zookeepers ran in to see what was the matter. One of them carefully walked up to the giant oyster, patted his shell reassuringly, and said, "Easy, now. It's me, Joe—remember?"

But Clamu was so upset, he gave out a mighty roar, grabbed Joe with his powerful tongue, and hurled him out of the stadium. Joe went flying like a rocket, screaming all the way.

Smiling, Patrick elbowed SpongeBob. "Now *this* is a show!" he said.

Clutching his bag of sea peanuts, SpongeBob looked worried.

Outside the stadium, a loudspeaker blared forth a warning to everybody: "Attention, zoo patrons! Clamu the Giant Oyster is on an emotional rampage! Please scream and run around in circles!"

Everyone screamed and ran around in circles. They even let go of their free balloons and let them float away. "Thanks for coming," said the friendly voice over the loudspeaker.

Back inside Oyster Stadium, Clamu was leaping around his pit, smashing into the walls and destroying everything in his way. He was also still crying very loudly.

Patrick and SpongeBob sat in the stands of

the stadium, watching. A zookeeper ran up to them. "You boys better get out of this area," he said. "Pronto!" He looked down at Clamu, who was still crashing around. "There's nothing more dangerous than an emotionally disturbed oyster."

Suddenly the zookeeper pointed an accusing finger at SpongeBob, who cowered behind his bag of sea peanuts. "*You* didn't do anything that might have caused this horrible tragedy, did you?" he asked.

"Uhhhhhhhh . . . ," said SpongeBob.

"No way!" said Patrick firmly. "Only a bully would upset a gentle giant." He turned to his friend. "Right, SpongeBob?"

SpongeBob looked down at his bag of sea peanuts and quickly hid them behind his back. "Right," he said. Then he bit his lower lip, knowing he had just lied.

chapter three

Still crying, Clamu ripped huge sheets of metal from the walls of his pit and shook them back and forth. SpongeBob and Patrick took the zookeeper's advice and left the stadium.

As they walked out of the zoo, people ran past them screaming. Smoke rose from Oyster Stadium, and even from other buildings in the zoo.

But Patrick wasn't scared—just mad. "Man,

if I ever see the guy who upset Clamu, I'll have a few choice words for him," he said angrily. "Words like *you* . . . and . . . *are* . . . and . . . *a bully!*"

Soon they reached SpongeBob's sidewalk. Patrick asked, "Are you *sure* you didn't see anything suspicious?"

"I already said I didn't, Patrick! Jeesh!" yelled SpongeBob, hurrying toward his front door.

This outburst didn't faze Patrick. He had an idea. "Hey!" he said excitedly. "Let's investigate this crime and catch the lowlife who's responsible."

Fed up—and feeling guilty—SpongeBob threw his hands into the air and waved them.

"Give it a rest, Patrick!" he shouted. "There is no crime to investigate! Now, go home!"

SpongeBob went into his house and slammed the door behind him. Then he leaned against it with his arms folded and frowned.

"Stupid Patrick," he said. "I didn't do anything wrong."

Trying to be his usual optimistic self, SpongeBob told himself that everything would be just fine.

"Aw, what am I getting so worked up about?" he asked, smiling. "I'm sure that by tomorrow this whole ugly mess will be a funny memory!"

Forcing out a little chuckle, he sat down

in his comfy life preserver chair to watch television. He settled back and clicked the remote.

The Bikini Bottom news came on. When he heard what the newscaster was saying, SpongeBob immediately sat upright in his chair.

"Our top story tonight: Giant Oyster Has Its Feelings Hurt!"

SpongeBob gulped as he saw Clamu on the screen, still crying.

"The only clue that could be found was this lone peanut," the newscaster continued.

The newscast showed a close-up of the very peanut SpongeBob had tossed at Clamu. SpongeBob just stared at the screen, horrified.

"And as you can hear," said the newscaster, "the oyster continues to emit its horrible cry— a cry so powerful it can be heard around the world!"

The TV showed pictures of people covering their ears all over the planet—in front of Egyptian pyramids, Dutch windmills, and the Taj Mahal in India.

"A cry that not only breaks the sound

barrier, it breaks the hearts of our citizens," said the newscaster as a Bikini Bottom mother and her two children sobbed by Clamu's pit.

SpongeBob could scarcely believe what he was seeing.

The newscaster finished his broadcast by asking, "What kind of cruel, careless, evil person would deliberately upset one of Neptune's gentlest creatures?"

A single tear dripped from the newscaster's eye, and a hand came in from off camera to wipe it away. SpongeBob couldn't take it anymore. He turned off the TV.

"Meow?" asked Gary, his pet snail.

 "AHHHHH!" screamed SpongeBob. But then he regained his composure and faced the pink snail. "No,

Gary!" he said forcefully. "How would I know anything about the oyster?"

Gary stared at SpongeBob with his two big eyes perched on top of their long eyestalks. "Meow," he said.

"Defensive?" cried SpongeBob. "I'm not being defensive!" He threw his hands up and looked at the ceiling. "Barnacles! What is this—Twenty Questions or something?"

As he strode away from Gary, SpongeBob heard Clamu's terrible loud cry. He peered out his window at Oyster Stadium, where the sobs were coming from.

"This is getting a little out of hand," he said, clutching his square head. "All I did was throw a peanut. I didn't mean to make the oyster cry! I just wanted to see it perform spectacular stunts!"

SpongeBob wrung his hands. "Aw, everyone's gonna hate me! I need some advice."

He thought hard for a minute. "Let's see now . . . who could *never* hate me no matter *what* I do?"

chapter four

"Squidward! Oh, Squuiid-waard!"

SpongeBob was pounding on his grouchy neighbor's front door. He was sure Squidward liked him so much that he could never hate him no matter what.

Rubbing his bald head, Squidward opened the door. "SpongeBob!" he growled. "Do you have to knock so loudly?"

"Sorry, neighbor," apologized SpongeBob.

At the zoo Clamu was crying louder than ever. Squidward rubbed his temples with his tentacles.

"Oh," he moaned. "That overgrown oyster is giving me a headache. I can't even take my afternoon beauty nap!"

SpongeBob laughed nervously. "Funny thing you should mention that old oyster . . ." For a second, he thought about telling Squidward the whole truth.

But then he saw Squidward frowning grumpily. SpongeBob decided that maybe he'd better be a little more indirect.

"Let's say I know this guy," he continued uneasily, "who *may* have something to do with the oyster crying."

Squidward looked thrilled.

"You mean you know the guy who upset Clamu?" he asked eagerly.

SpongeBob swallowed hard with a loud gulp.

"Oh, this is great!" exclaimed Squidward. "You and I can go turn him in. And then I'll get so much sleep, I'll be gorgeous!"

This was *not* the reaction SpongeBob had been hoping for. "Uh, actually I'm just talking hypothetically," he said.

Squidward's big smile immediately dropped into a frown. "You mean you don't know who did it?" he asked.

"Well, eeh, uh, I . . . ," SpongeBob stammered, unsure what to say. He didn't really like to lie. But Squidward obviously was going to turn him in to the authorities if he told the truth. "No," he finally said.

Squidward slammed the door, loudly, in SpongeBob's face.

"Squidward?" asked SpongeBob. Sighing, he turned and walked away . . . right into Patrick!

"GOTCHA!" said Patrick, wearing a detective's hat and staring through a magnifying glass.

"AHHHH!" screamed SpongeBob.

But Patrick didn't seem to be speaking to SpongeBob. He was looking through his magnifying glass at something tiny on the boardwalk to Squidward's house.

"Where were you on the day of today?" he asked accusingly. "Don't play games with me, mister!"

"Hey, Patrick," said SpongeBob. "What are you doing?"

Patrick looked up from his magnifying glass

and noticed SpongeBob for the first time. "Oh hi, SpongeBob!" he said cheerfully. "I'm just continuing my investigation of the Zoo Day Disaster!"

SpongeBob's right eye started to twitch. "Um . . ." he said, afraid to ask. "Have you found out anything?"

"Yes!" exclaimed Patrick confidently. Then

he scratched his head. "No, wait . . . um . . . no." He picked up a tiny grain of sand. "But this grain of sand looks pretty suspicious. And so does this rock! And I've got a few questions for this little piece of grass!"

Panting and sweating, SpongeBob ran away, holding his elbows high.

Patrick called after him, "Don't worry, SpongeBob! Patrick's on the case! THE TRUTH WILL BE REVEALED!"

SpongeBob kept running, thinking, I'd better go see Sandy. She'll know what to do!

chapter five

Sandy Cheeks, Bikini Bottom's only land squirrel, stood with her fingers stuffed in her ears. She was trying to block out the sound of Clamu's anguished cries, but it wasn't working.

"Ohhhh," she cried. "I can't stand it anymore! That poor, poor critter! What kind of inconsiderate person would upset such a gentle creature?"

Wearing a water-filled helmet, SpongeBob sat on a log in Sandy's treedome, tracing a little circle on the log with his finger.

"That's kind of what I wanted to talk to you about, Sandy . . . ," he began. But Sandy interrupted him, speaking angrily with her fists clenched tightly at her sides.

"Why, when I find out who caused that oyster so much pain," she shouted, "no more jiggery-pokery!" Sandy was so mad, she ripped a copy of the Bikini Bottom phone book right in half.

"Now," she said, calming herself, "what was it you wanted to talk about, SpongeBob?"

SpongeBob was so scared by Sandy's incredible display of angry strength that he

couldn't speak. "Ooh, I, *ee*, uh, ooh, ahh, *ee*, uh, ooh," he babbled, squinting his right eye and twisting his fingers.

Sandy looked puzzled. "Hey, SpongeBob," she asked, "how come you're all twitchy like that?"

SpongeBob sat on the log, vibrating.

"Twitchy? Twitchy?" he managed to bleat out. "Who's twitchy? I'm not twitchy!"

He jumped to his feet. He had to get out of there! He came up with a quick excuse. "Sorry, Sandy," he said. "I have to . . . uh . . . go get my hair cut!"

SpongeBob ran out of the treedome. Rubbing her chin, Sandy watched him go. "SpongeBob doesn't have hair. Or does he?" she wondered.

Frightened that everyone would find out he'd thrown the peanut, SpongeBob ran straight to his pineapple house. But before he could get the front door open, Patrick walked up.

"Hey, SpongeBob!" called Patrick.

SpongeBob was so startled, he collapsed on his front doorstep. As he got up, Patrick rubbed his hands together and said, "This is it! All the clues are coming together!"

Patrick bent over a trail of shoeprints in the

sand leading to SpongeBob's front door. "I followed these footprints right to this exact spot!" he said. SpongeBob looked very worried.

"And then," Patrick continued, "right where you're standing, I found this bag of peanuts! Ha!"

He held up a red-striped bag of sea peanuts. SpongeBob gritted his teeth and shook with fear.

"Oh," gloated Patrick, "I'm so close to solving this crime, I can almost taste it!"

"Okay, uh, good luck with all that, Patrick. And, uh, I guess

I'll see you later," said SpongeBob, trying to sound innocent. He slipped inside his front door and slammed it behind him, leaving Patrick outside.

Inside his house SpongeBob just stood there trembling. Suddenly someone banged on the door.

"OPEN UP! THIS IS THE POLICE!"

chapter six

When he heard the police, SpongeBob was so terrified that his eyeballs popped out of his head and rolled across the floor.

"Uh, just a second!" he said in a high voice as he groped around, trying to find his eyes.

The two policemen opened the door, flashing their badges. "Are you SpongeBob SquarePants?" they asked.

SpongeBob just stood there holding his

eyeballs in his hands. "Y—y—yes," he managed to say.

"Put those eyeballs back in your head, son! We've got a few questions for you!" one of the policemen barked.

SpongeBob popped his eyes back in his head and spun them around with his fingers until they were in the right position. Blinking, he looked up at the tall policemen.

"Were you at the zoo on the day of the oyster incident?" asked the policeman in front. His partner stood silently behind him, patting his flipper with his nightstick.

"Yes," SpongeBob admitted, sinking into his collar.

"Did you or did you not take part in various activities of zoo-time merriment?" the policeman asked sternly.

SpongeBob sank even farther into his square clothes. "Yes," he squeaked.

The policeman held up a peanut in a plastic bag labeled EXHIBIT A.

"And are you familiar with *this peanut*?" the policeman demanded to know.

"Yes!" whimpered SpongeBob, sinking so far into his clothes that he ripped out the bottom of his pants. His underpants hit the floor with a *CLANG*!

"Just one more question," said the policeman. SpongeBob stood there shaking, biting his nails, sure that the policeman was about to ask him if

he'd thrown the peanut at Clamu. What would the punishment be for such a terrible crime?

"Is it true that you were at the oyster's lair with a Mr. Patrick Star?" asked the policeman.

"Yes!" wailed SpongeBob. "Yes! It's all true! The merriment! The peanut! The Patrick!" He fell to his knees, crying.

"That's all we need to know, son," said the policeman, satisfied. He turned to his partner. "Let's book him!"

Just then Patrick came in and stood behind his friend. SpongeBob was all ready to be arrested, but then the policemen slapped handcuffs on Patrick!

"Wow, you guys are good!" exclaimed Patrick. "I'm the *last* person I would have suspected! But I was looking for me all the time! It's the perfect crime!"

"Yeah, yeah, tell it to the judge, pinkie," growled the policeman as he led Patrick out in the handcuffs.

Stunned, SpongeBob watched the officers put Patrick in their police boat. He couldn't believe they were taking his best friend to jail. "Oh, no!" he cried. "Patrick's too sensitive for the big house!"

As the police boat sped off with its siren wailing, SpongeBob chased after it.

"Wait! Stop!" he called, pulling up his pants. "*I'm* the one you want! I AM THE CRIMINAL!"

chapter seven

"Booooooooo!" jeered the crowd. Oyster Stadium was full of angry Bikini Bottomers. They had all come to see the mean bully who had upset Clamu.

In Clamu's arena, the giant oyster was still crying. Patrick stood on top of a half-sunken barrel to which his arms were chained. He was trying to ignore the Bikini Bottomers who were yelling at him.

One especially angry dweller spoke up, raising his voice above the noise of the crowd. "Hey, everybody!" he yelled. "Let's throw peanuts at him and see how he likes it!"

Everyone started hurling peanuts at Patrick. "I get what I deserve," he said bravely.

Patrick caught several peanuts in his mouth and swallowed them. Since they were still in their shells, this wasn't a very good idea. "Ouch," he said.

Just then, SpongeBob rushed into the arena.

"Wait!" he shouted. The crowd hushed. "Hold your peanuts! Patrick Star is innocent!"

SpongeBob strode purposefully forward into the center of the arena and looked up at the angry mob. "I have come here to reveal the truth!" he said.

He took a deep breath and began the speech he had planned on his way to Oyster Stadium. "They say that truth and honesty will be rewarded with trust and forgiveness."

Realizing that SpongeBob was delivering one of his heartfelt speeches, Patrick started to sing a slow, respectful anthem in the background. He couldn't think of any words, so he just sang, "Bum, bum-bum-bum, bum, bum."

"I'm here to lay my cards on the table," SpongeBob continued earnestly. "To trim the branches of deception from the tree of life. To shave away the unkempt sideburns from the face of truth! I—"

"Oh, just get on with it!" screamed the guy who had suggested throwing peanuts at Patrick.

It was now or never. SpongeBob closed his eyes and said, "I am the one who threw the peanut."

The crowd roared its disapproval. But SpongeBob raised his hand, letting them know he had more to say.

"I know now that what I have done is wrong," he stated in a clear, strong voice. "And so I say, I am sorry, giant performing oyster!"

He walked over to Clamu and placed his hand gently on its shell. Then he turned to Patrick, who was still singing his solemn anthem.

"I am sorry, Patrick."

SpongeBob turned back to the crowd in the stadium and raised both his hands. "I am sorry, citizens of Bikini Bottom."

For a moment it was very still in Oyster Stadium. Even Patrick stopped singing, and the giant oyster stopped sobbing. SpongeBob was sure everyone was going to forgive him.

Then a voice rang out. "Hey, let's throw peanuts at *both* of them!" cried the guy who had thought of throwing peanuts in the first place. The crowd agreed, yelling angrily.

"Wait!" shouted a zookeeper. "Here's the *real* criminal!" He dragged Mr. Krabs, who was still wearing his fake mustache, into the arena.

"Uh . . . top o' the mornin'!" said Mr. Krabs, trying to keep up his brilliant disguise. But when he spoke, his black mustache fell off.

"Mr. Krabs!" exclaimed SpongeBob, shocked.

The crowd of citizens gasped.

"I knew it!" shouted Patrick.

"Mr. Krabs has stolen a very important item from the oyster!" announced the zookeeper. "Behold!"

The zookeeper held up Mr. Krabs's clothing, which he'd just yanked off by accident.

Everyone in the stadium covered their eyes, muttering things like "Ew" and "Yuck."

"Wait a minute," said the zookeeper. He gave Mr. Krabs his clothes back and hoisted a shiny, round, white object high in the air. "Behold! The oyster's pearl!"

Everyone gasped.

The zookeeper took the pearl over to Clamu and set it on the ground, saying, "Here you go!" Then he tipped his hat to the giant oyster and backed away respectfully.

Clamu sniffed the pearl and seemed to

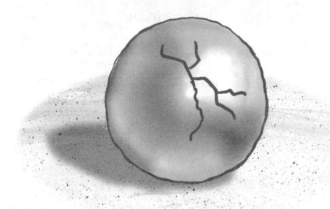

recognize it. Everyone except Mr. Krabs cheered. They were happy that the oyster had his pearl back.

But just as they were all cheering, the pearl started to crack!

chapter eight

Tiny crack lines appeared all over the surface of the beautiful pearl. The crowd gasped in horror. What would the giant oyster do if Mr. Krabs had somehow broken its beloved pearl? Would it go on a rampage, destroying all of Bikini Bottom?

The pearl fell completely apart and . . . a little baby oyster popped out! "Mama, mama!" it cried.

"Mother of pearl!" said SpongeBob, beaming. "The oyster's a mother!" Everyone now realized that Clamu was a girl, not a boy. "And that pearl's no pearl," he explained. "It's an egg!"

He was right. The shiny ball that everyone had assumed was a pearl was actually Clamu's egg. And now the giant oyster had a baby oyster all its own!

The baby swam over to its gigantic mother and warbled, "Mama!" again. Clamu greeted her baby, who immediately jumped up on

Clamu's back. Clamu smiled. She and her baby clearly loved each other.

"Awwww," sighed the crowd, enjoying the touching moment between oyster and child.

Then everyone turned their heads and glared at Mr. Krabs, who had stolen the egg in the first place, upsetting Clamu and making her cry so loud and long.

Mr. Krabs shrugged. "But it's Free Day!" he protested feebly as the crowd covered him in peanuts.

about the author

David Lewman has written more than thirty-five books for children, including titles based on the television shows *The Fairly OddParents*, *The Adventures of Jimmy Neutron*, *Rugrats*, *Teenage Mutant Ninja Turtles*, and *SpongeBob SquarePants*. He has also written for TV shows such as MTV's *3-South* and Comedy Central's *Drawn Together*.

David lives in Sherman Oaks, California.